DRAGONS, DRACULA AND DINOSAURS

BOOK SIX

STEPHANIE BAUDET

Published by Sweet Cherry Publishing Limited
Unit 36, Vulcan House
Vulcan Road
Leicester, LE5 3EF
United Kingdom

www.sweetcherrypublishing.com

First published in the UK in 2016
2020 edition

ISBN: 978-1-78226-270-1

Illustrations © Allied Artists
Illustrated by Illary Casasanta
Cover design by Andrew Davis

The Dinosaur Detectives: Dragons, Dracula and Dinosaurs

Printed and bound in India
I.IPP001

CHAPTER ONE

The creature was immense. Matt gasped and took a step back. The weight of the fossilised egg he was holding faded away as he became more involved in the vision. This was one he might have chosen to step out of, except that he didn't have a choice. Ever since Matt was six he had had an amazing ability to see dinosaurs as they would have appeared when they were alive. It happened spontaneously when he was holding the egg of that particular species.

Strictly speaking, this wasn't a dinosaur. He knew that. Matt knew an awful lot about dinosaurs because his father, Alan Sharp, was an eminent palaeontologist.

The animal that stood before him was a type of pterosaur, or flying prehistoric creature. This

was a Hatzegopteryx and it towered about five metres above him, twice the height of a normal house ceiling. Its body was grey and its long neck orange. Above that, a terrifying sharp beak protruded almost two metres from its head. More importantly, at that moment it was pointing towards him. This was what had made Matt step back, although he knew that it could not see him.

The creature stood on its hind feet. Outstretched, its wings would span eleven

metres, but they were currently folded. The Hatzegopteryx was using the joints in its wings like elbows, which gave the impression that it had four legs. These 'elbows' also had clawed feet on the end, and so were multifunctional. Matt was near enough to touch the leathery wings and couldn't resist reaching out his hand towards them, although he'd never been able to touch anything in visions before. He could now smell his environment and even turn around within the scene, so he could have a look around. He could feel the air too: right now it was warm and steamy.

As his fingers touched the cold, tough flesh of the wing, Matt jumped back again. This was new! Now he could touch things. Where would this end? With each vision he gained an extra sense and he could now use four of his five senses, though he couldn't begin to imagine how taste could be involved. What if, eventually, he would actually be there? He shuddered at the thought.

Matt looked up at the Hatzegopteryx. Fortunately it didn't seem to be aware of him and hadn't reacted to his touch. Heart pounding, he tentatively touched the wing again and then its leg. That was scaly and tough. Wow! thought Matt, I am the only person EVER to have touched a living prehistoric creature. He could hardly believe what was happening.

As the vision faded Matt found himself back in his living room at home with his dad looking at him in anticipation, paintbrush poised over his watercolour palette. Matt's dad was a famous palaeo-artist and his paintings of prehistoric creatures were sought-after all around the world. People were beginning to question the source of

his knowledge, but so far Matt and his family had decided to keep quiet about Matt's visions.

Matt looked at the light sketch his dad had drawn already. 'The beak's longer and a sort of dull yellow. The neck is orange, and, Dad – I touched it! I can feel things now! How amazing is that?'

Mr Sharp stopped painting and turned to look at his son. 'You are very privileged, Matt.'

Matt frowned.

'What is it, Matt? You look worried.'

'Where will it end? Will I eventually really be there?'

Matt could tell that the thought had crossed his Dad's mind too. If he was there, would the dinosaurs see him?

'I really don't know,' said Dad with a worried frown. 'In the meantime … this Hatzegopteryx egg was found in Romania, and I've just been in touch with some experts who want me to go out there.'

Matt jumped up. 'Really? And are Jo and I coming too?'

Jo was Matt's cousin. Her parents were busy doctors and Jo had accompanied them on the last five fossil hunts. In fact, she had joined them ever since Matt had turned twelve, a year ago, and first been allowed to accompany his dad during school holidays.

Dad was looking at him intently. 'How do you feel about Jo always joining us, Matt? I know how much you'd looked forward to it being just you and me.'

Matt smiled ruefully. 'It's true, Dad, I did really resent it at first but I've got used to her now, and actually she can be fun to be with.'

Mr Sharp patted his son's shoulder. 'I'm glad,' he said. 'I was worried at first. You didn't seem very happy about it, and bringing two children along with me can look a little unprofessional.'

'It's definitely been more exciting with Jo around,' Matt said. 'Will we be looking for Hatzegopteryx in Romania?'

His dad shook his head. 'It's a different kind of expedition this time. There has been a theft of dinosaur eggs from an excavation site in the north of the country, and it's obviously someone who knows what he's doing. An expert. Someone who wants to gain financially by selling them to a collector. Does anyone spring to mind?'

'Frank Hellman,' said Matt, without hesitation.

His dad nodded. 'They think, by the description, that it's him. He was seen hanging around the site.'

Matt pulled a face. Frank Hellman had been a fellow student of his dad's at university and saw Mr Sharp as a rival. He had pursued them on the last five expeditions, ruthlessly trying to steal the eggs they found. He didn't need the money, but he had no real interest in palaeontology either. All Hellman wanted was the fame and prestige, and to get one up on Dad. The resentment and jealousy was part of an ongoing feud between the two men's families.

'Because I know him, they think I may be able to think like he does and work out how he'll smuggle the eggs out of the country. They are already watching the airports and railway stations, but some of the remoter border crossings are more difficult to monitor.'

'I hope we catch him,' said Matt emphatically.

CHAPTER TWO

A week later, they were all in Bucharest: Matt, his dad and Jo. Matt's mum and sister, Beth, never came with them. Neither of them had any interest in dinosaurs.

It was late October but the sun still had some warmth to it. Matt sighed with pleasure. This would be an interesting mission, with the opportunity of getting the better of Frank Hellman too. Somebody had to stop him stealing fossils: having to look behind themselves all the time spoilt the fun of their expeditions. Not only that, but if they recovered the stolen eggs, Matt would be able to have another vision too.

'Have you come up with any plans, Uncle Alan?' said Jo as they got into the taxi to go to

their hotel, taking the words right out of Matt's mouth.

'I have been doing some thinking,' said Mr Sharp. 'The Romanians are keeping a watch on airports and railway stations. My guess is that he'll try to get out by road through a remote border, perhaps into Hungary. But we mustn't underestimate Frank. He'll know they're after him and he's not stupid.'

'He doesn't know that we're after him, though, Dad,' Matt said thoughtfully.

'No, and I'm hoping it doesn't get leaked to the press.'

'Can't you think about how you would smuggle the eggs out, Uncle Alan?' asked Jo.

Mr Sharp shook his head. 'That's just it. I have to think about how Frank would do it. That's why I have been invited: I know Frank.'

But the look on his dad's face told Matt that maybe he didn't know Frank that well and trying to get into his mindset wasn't working so far.

'What kind of dinosaur eggs has he stolen?'

With all the excitement of packing, Matt hadn't asked the obvious question and now Jo had beaten him to it. Her thought processes seemed to have run along the same lines as his own.

'They were from a small dinosaur called Balaur bondoc, named after a dragon in Romanian mythology,' said Dad. 'It was only about two metres long but it was a powerful carnivore. In the late Cretaceous period, the region of Romania where it roamed was an island, and it's thought that Balaur was the biggest beast on the island. Its fossils have only been found in Romania.'

'The eggs wouldn't be very big then, Dad,' said Matt. 'Easy for the thief to carry away.'

Mr Sharp shook his head. 'It was a whole nest, so it will be quite heavy. I'm more and more convinced that the only way he could get it out would be by road.'

'Haven't they got CCTV in the museum? And were they just lying there? I can't see how anyone could steal something like that.' Jo was frowning.

'No, they were taken straight from the dig site.'

Matt looked at his dad. 'Sounds like Frank Hellman. This time he followed someone else instead of you, Dad.'

Mr Sharp looked at his watch distractedly. 'I'm meeting someone at the Natural History Museum here once we've dropped our bags off. It's called the Grigore Antipa Museum. I think you'll find it interesting. Maybe you two can look around while I meet the man in charge of the investigation.'

Matt nodded. It was always fun to look around a new museum.

The Grigore Antipa Museum was a long, pale yellow building with a grand columned portico over the main entrance.

As they walked in, they were met by a man who spoke perfect English, and indicated that Mr Sharp should go with him.

Matt's dad looked back over his shoulder as he followed the man. 'Amuse yourselves, you two. I'll find you when the meeting is over.'

Matt nodded, looking around. He couldn't wait to start exploring. The palaeontology exhibits were on the first floor and, without a word, he and Jo automatically made for the stairs.

The first room they looked into took Matt's breath away as he stepped inside. 'Wow!' he whispered, almost to himself.

Around the walls were large illuminated tableaux of stuffed animals in their natural habitats, but the thing that had captured Matt's attention was a huge skeleton in the centre of the room.

'What is it?' asked Jo, stepping forward to look at the plaque. 'Deinotherium giganteum,' she read. 'Well, it's certainly giganteum.' She laughed.

Matt didn't recognise it at all. 'It's not a dinosaur.'

They found the English translation. It certainly wasn't a dinosaur. It was an enormous mammoth-like creature that had lived in the late Miocene epoch, about twenty million years ago. It was seven metres long, around four metres high and weighed approximately 13,000 kilograms.

Jo smiled at Matt. 'Awesome!' she said. 'Would your dad be interested even though it's not a dinosaur?'

'Of course!' Matt turned to look at her. 'It's still prehistoric and interesting to palaeontologists, it's just that Dad specialises in fossilised dinosaur eggs and this was a mammal. They don't lay eggs.'

Jo gave him a friendly punch on the arm. 'I do know that, Matt.'

'Sorry.'

That was as far as they got with their exploration. Half an hour later Matt's dad found them in the same room, still poring over the exhibits.

'Dad, look!' Matt gestured to the massive creature in the middle of the room. 'This is the only one that was ever found intact.'

But to both Matt's and Jo's surprise, Mr Sharp hardly glanced at the skeleton dominating the room.

'Come on! We have to rent a car and head north. Frank Hellman has been spotted!'

CHAPTER THREE

Matt didn't have a chance to ask any questions. When his dad was like this, it was best to just keep quiet. They were whisked to a car hire place and before they knew it they were on the road towards Transylvania, or so his dad had muttered. Matt could see by his dad's face that he wanted to get on Frank Hellman's trail as soon as possible. If it even was Frank Hellman.

After some miles of sitting and staring at the landscape, Matt ventured, 'Dad, you didn't see the …'

'The Deinotherium giganteum?'

Matt nodded.

'I know it's there; it's unique. Maybe when we get back we can revisit the museum.'

Dad really wants to get Frank Hellman, Matt thought. But was he doing it to recover the eggs, or to get back at Hellman? Matt wasn't sure. Whichever it was, Dad must have had a powerful motive to resist going to see that awesome skeleton.

'How do they know it's Hellman who's been seen?' asked Jo, obviously deciding that it was safe to speak now too.

'He fits the description. The police have been keeping a lookout for strangers, particularly in remoter areas, and they have a whole team of people helping them. The area where he's been seen, if it is him, is not particularly touristic. There's one strange thing, though ...'

Both Matt and Jo waited expectantly.

'... This man was asking about wolves.'

'Wolves?' It hadn't occurred to Matt that there were any wolves in Romania.

His dad read his mind. 'There are wolves here, and brown bears,' he said. 'Both species are protected, but people still hunt them although it's illegal. There is an annual quota of wolves that can legally be shot though.'

'I read about that!' said Jo.

Matt frowned. Jo was a bit of a know-all sometimes, but he supposed he couldn't complain that she didn't do any research before an expedition, even if it wasn't always about dinosaurs.

Jo turned to face Matt. 'They are rarely seen, but wolves are a central part of Romania's forest ecosystem. By keeping down the numbers of deer and wild boar, they allow new trees and vegetation to grow and this provides habitats for birds and other animals.'

Jo sounded as though she was quoting from an online source. Matt guessed this was going to be her project for their expedition. He had to admire her, though. Every time they went anywhere, Jo seemed to find a new topic to capture her interest. She didn't get bored with it when she got home either, but seemed seriously concerned about each one.

Soon there were low-lying hills on either side of the road and they followed a river on their right for miles. Slivers of sun flashed through the trees.

Dad seemed to have calmed down a little from his earlier agitated state, realising that they couldn't possibly get there any quicker.

'Are we in Transylvania, Uncle Alan?' asked Jo.

Mr Sharp nodded.

'Dracula country,' she said, with relish. 'Where's his castle?'

'The one attributed to him is in Bran, further east of here,' said her uncle.

'He wasn't real,' Matt said.

'I know, but it's still a good story.'

'Dracul,' said Mr Sharp, 'was a chivalrous award given to aristocrats. It refers to The Order of the Dragon. In old Romanian, Dracul meant dragon, although in modern Romanian it means "devil". The modern word for "dragon" is Balaur, which is the name of our little dinosaur.'

He had hardly finished talking when a loud bang came from underneath them and the car slewed across the road. Mr Sharp grappled with the steering wheel, trying to bring it under control.

If another car came along at this moment … Matt and Jo clung on to their seats for dear life. Matt could feel his heart thumping as fear gripped him: they were going to have a terrible accident, out here in a remote part of Romania!

Finally, after what seemed like minutes but was actually only a few seconds, his dad brought the car to a stop on the grass between the road and the river. They were all silent for a few moments, in shock. Matt stared out at the swirling river not a metre away from his door.

'Are you both all right?' His dad's voice was unsteady and came out as a hoarse whisper as he turned around to look at them.

'Yes, Dad.' Matt looked at Jo, who could only nod.

'I think we had a blowout.'

It was dusk and there hadn't been any passing traffic for some time. The sun was setting behind the hills on their left and the trees had taken on a dark, ominous air.

Mr Sharp got out of the car, staggered over to the front wheel and then nodded, poking his head back inside. 'A puncture.'

Matt and Jo got out shakily as Dad opened the boot and lifted out their luggage. Before long, he had found the jack and the wheel spanner and

laid them on the ground. Under a flap he found the spare wheel and lifted that out too, only to groan in dismay.

'What's wrong, Dad?'

'It's flat. The spare wheel is flat.' He looked around as if he'd only just noticed the remoteness of their location. 'We're stuck.'

CHAPTER FOUR

The trio hadn't noticed the sky cloud over. But as they stared at their surroundings, they realised that a low cloud had descended onto the hills; tendrils of thick mist were drifting into the valley. Mr Sharp stared into the boot as though it might conjure up another wheel. Eventually he turned despondently towards Matt and Jo.

'I'm sorry, but we might have to sleep in the car.'

Matt and Jo looked around. The wind had a chill to it now that the sun was setting. 'It's all that talk about Dracula,' he said. He was trying to make a joke, but he could see why Bram Stoker had set his novel here. It was a creepy feeling, having the mist swirl around them like this.

'Come on. Let's be ready in case someone comes along,' said his dad. 'If we can flag them

down, they're bound to understand. "Hotel" is a universal word and it's obvious what has happened to us. If we can get a lift to a hotel, I'll call a garage tomorrow.'

They all stood and stared at the empty road, doing their best to feel hopeful. Matt tried to remember how long it had been since they'd passed the last town of any size.

A sudden mournful sound rose out of the darkness nearby and echoed around the hills. Then another. And another. The sound sent shivers down Matt's spine. He'd never heard anything like it before, but he knew what it was.

So did Dad and Jo.

Wolves.

At the same time there came another sound, and they all looked up as a vehicle loomed out of the mist, travelling in the same direction as they had been. It was a wagon pulled by two coal-black horses. The noise they had heard was the sound of the horses' hooves gently clip-clopping along the road. The driver was a tall man, his face partly hidden by a huge black hat. As he approached and slowed down he lifted his head a fraction. Matt saw his dark eyes. He was not smiling.

'Our car has a flat tyre,' said Dad, pointing to it. 'Could you take us to a hotel please?' He repeated the word slowly as if he was talking to someone who was hard of hearing. 'Hoooo-telllll.'

The man's expression didn't change but he nodded and pointed to Dad and the seat beside him, then to Matt and Jo and the back of the cart. They got the message and began to clamber in. The back was empty except for a large wooden crate.

Dad hauled the suitcases up into the cart without any help from the man. As soon as they were all aboard, the driver cracked his whip and they were off, swaying this way and that. Matt and Jo clung tightly to the sides to stop themselves from being thrown about.

They looked at each other, both slightly panicked, wondering if getting a lift from this stranger had been a good idea. Once, Dad looked back at them and raised his eyebrows as if to ask if they were okay.

The cart slowed. Maybe we're there, thought Matt, although he couldn't see any lights or buildings. The wind was rising; it shrieked and moaned through the swaying trees.

As the clouds cleared and the moon came out, the wolves began to howl again, making the horses skitter about nervously. Finally, the driver was forced to stop.

They all looked at each other wordlessly. Matt was sure his dad was worried about where the driver was taking them, but they had no alternative: they could either trust him or be left stuck by the side of a road in the middle of nowhere, surrounded by wolves.

They watched the driver standing in front of the horses, whispering soothingly and stroking their trembling necks until they quietened. Then he silently climbed back into his seat and they were off again.

After another twenty minutes, they saw the shape of a building up ahead. It looked like a castle, with huge crenelated turrets and battlements forming a grim silhouette against the moonlit sky. There were lights on in the right wing but the left side was dark.

Jo grabbed his arm. 'I wish I hadn't mentioned Dracula,' she said with a nervous giggle.

The man did help them out of the cart, then he pointed at the door. For the first time, he spoke. 'Hotel,' he said emphatically. He got back onto his cart, gave a crack of the whip, and clattered off into the darkness.

It didn't look much like a hotel, although there was a faded sign above the door that was impossible to read, but they had no choice. Dad walked towards the stone porch, lifted the heavy knocker, and banged on the great wooden door.

The sound seemed to resonate through the building. They heard muffled footsteps and a key turning in the lock, then the door swung open creakily.

Framed in the doorway, there stood a big man with a large black moustache and shoulder-length hair. When he saw them, he stepped back and made a sweeping gesture with his hand to indicate that they should enter.

Despite its gloomy outward appearance,

the great hall of the castle looked warm and welcoming. Although the stone walls could have looked cold and forbidding, the soft lighting and red carpet made the interior feel almost homely, Matt thought. The contrast was almost unsettling in itself.

'Welcome to my hotel,' the man said, in perfect, unaccented English. Matt wondered how he had known that they were English.

'Our car got a flat tyre and the spare was flat too,' explained Dad, wearily.

The man nodded. 'How inconvenient,' he said.

The great hall had a high ceiling and a flagged stone floor. Doors on both sides led off from the room, and an enormous ornate gilded mirror hung on the left-hand wall. A stone staircase rose from the centre and they followed the man up, along a passage, and into a large room with a welcoming log fire.

'Your room, sirs,' he said to Mr Sharp and Matt. Then he looked at Jo. 'Your room is next door, Miss.'

Jo looked a little apprehensive, but followed him.

Later they were served a meal. They sat alone in a vast dining room as there didn't seem to be any other guests staying there with them. Matt found this a little strange, although he supposed that it was in a remote place and perhaps it was no longer the holiday season.

An alarming thought crossed his mind. What if there were traps set for travellers so that they were left stranded? Then the unfriendly man in the cart could drive along, pick them up, and bring them here. For a commission, of course.

Matt shook his head. He was letting his imagination run away with him.

But how come the fire in their room had already been lit?

'What is it?' asked Jo.

'Silly things,' said Matt. He frowned: the owner of the hotel hadn't seemed at all surprised to see them.

'Dracula again?'

'Something like that.' Matt grinned, trying to dispel the thought. 'I wonder if we're allowed to explore?'

He had noticed that the bedrooms, guests' lounge and dining room were all on one side of the castle.

When they asked, the man shook his head. 'That's private,' he said gruffly. 'My house.'

Matt would have believed him and thought no more about it if he hadn't seen something strange later on.

They were having a walk around the grounds before going to bed. The mist was starting to dissipate, although wisps still lingered, making the castle seem all the more eerie in its cold grandeur.

As they passed near one of the windows of the private wing, a light was switched on and off again very quickly. But it wasn't quite rapid enough. Matt caught a glimpse inside and it certainly didn't look like the room of a private apartment.

In that brief moment Matt had seen something very familiar: a dinosaur skeleton. Not something people usually had in their living room.

CHAPTER FIVE

There hadn't been time to say anything or nudge Jo and draw her attention to the contents of the room, but Matt was sure of what he'd seen. Very little could be mistaken for a huge skeleton except, perhaps, a strange sculpture. He didn't mention it to his dad: he didn't have any proof of what he'd seen, after all, and he wasn't entirely sure he'd be taken seriously. But as they came back into the great hall, Matt glanced at the sturdy wooden door on his left.

'I saw something,' he said quietly to Jo. Dad had gone on ahead.

Jo turned as she was about to climb the stairs.

'Through that door,' Matt whispered. 'There's a dinosaur skeleton.'

Jo giggled. 'Matt, don't be silly! You're obsessed with them.' Then her expression changed as she saw his face. 'You're serious.'

Matt indicated that they should go into her room to talk.

'Someone flicked the light on and off quickly,' he said as they closed the door. 'It was unmistakeable. There was a tall dinosaur skeleton, although I could only see the head because the windows are so high.'

'Why would anyone have a fossil standing around in their home?'

There was a hint of scepticism in her voice and Matt felt himself getting rattled. He'd hoped that Jo, at least, would believe him. After all their travels together, surely by now she knew that he wasn't one to joke around.

'His own private collection?' suggested Matt. 'Where do you think Frank Hellman sells his stolen fossils?'

Jo shrugged. 'I just thought they had stashed them away in drawers, not on display like a museum.'

'Whatever,' said Matt. 'We should go and have a look. Maybe this is the end of the trail and Hellman sold the nest of eggs to this man. He could be back in England already.'

There was no hesitation on Jo's part. Her eyes gleamed with excitement. That's what Matt liked about her – she wasn't afraid of a little adventure, although he knew that what they planned to do was wrong.

But how were they going to get into the room? Presumably it was locked.

Meanwhile, Dad had tried to phone the car hire people who would be able to contact a garage to come and fix the tyre. The phone signal had been spasmodic, and Dad had realised that he didn't actually know where they were.

He went downstairs again to ask but there was no sign of the owner.

'We'll have to wait until morning,' he said resignedly. 'I can't believe this!'

Matt waited until his dad was asleep before creeping out of bed and pulling on his jeans and jacket. He quietly let himself out of the room and tapped on Jo's door.

'You still haven't told me how we're going to get through a locked door,' she said as she emerged from her room.

Matt had no idea. Maybe it wasn't even locked.

The landing was dimly lit. They crept carefully to the top of the stairs. No-one. Silence. Just the sound of his pounding heartbeat. At least there was no chance of the stone stairs creaking.

Matt gently tried the door handle. It didn't budge. It was locked. Of course it was.

They stared at it. There was nothing to do but go back to their rooms.

They had just reached the top of the stairs again when they heard a noise and both stopped, frozen to the spot. It was the sound of a key turning in a lock and a door opening. The door didn't exactly creak, as you might expect in an old castle, but there was a kind of sigh as the air shifted.

Matt and Jo looked at each other and ran to the landing. Reflected in the huge mirror was a man walking across the hall. Although the light was dim, his way of moving and his shape were unmistakeable. Frank Hellman!

He began to climb the stairs. They couldn't see him now, but he made no attempt to walk quietly and his footsteps echoed around the hall. Matt and Jo shrank back into the shadows, too late to escape into Jo's room. Hellman reached the top of the stairs and thankfully turned towards the rooms on the other side of the building.

Matt looked meaningfully at Jo. Hellman hadn't locked the door behind him. Or at least, they hadn't heard it lock.

They gave Hellman a minute or so to get into his room before hurrying down the stairs again. Matt grasped the door handle. This time it turned easily, with just a slight sound of wood against wood.

Moonlight streamed in through the tall Gothic windows casting weird shadows round the walls of the room.

Matt heard Jo gasp behind him as she stepped into the room and saw what he saw. It was an immense space with glass cases all around the walls, but what immediately caught their eye was the great skeleton in the centre of the room.

It was not as big as the Deinotherium giganteum they'd seen in Bucharest, but it was certainly more unexpected. And this one was a dinosaur. That much Matt knew. He didn't know what kind exactly, but it was definitely a carnivore judging by its large head and teeth. Its lower jaw hung down as though it was about to snap at some poor creature and crush it with its terrifying teeth.

They shut the door quietly and then slowly walked around the exhibits. Neither of them spoke. Matt had never seen a private collection of fossils, but here was one he wouldn't mind having. He couldn't help thinking that it was

unfair, though, to keep them hidden away from everyone else and not share them with the world.

There was another door at the far end and Matt wondered if it led to more rooms of collections. He tried it, but it was locked. As he turned away from it he heard a distinct sound. One that made his heart pound.

It was the sound of a key turning in the lock of the door through which they had entered.

Matt felt a sick feeling in the pit of his stomach and he saw the horror in Jo's eyes.

They were trapped.

CHAPTER SIX

'My phone!' whispered Jo, taking it out of her pocket.

'Who are you going to call?' asked Matt incredulously, struggling to keep his voice down.

'Your dad, of course.'

But there was no signal. No matter where she went in the room, nothing registered.

Just to make sure the door was locked, Matt tried it, but it didn't budge. He looked at Jo. 'Any ideas?'

She looked around, very carefully, her gaze lingering on every aspect of the room. It stopped at the windows.

'Too much noise,' said Matt.

'So what?'

'Last resort. We're not supposed to be in here, remember?'

Undeterred, Jo was already climbing up onto a glass case. Matt was scared to watch her – how much weight could those glass panels take? If the case broke, she would be seriously hurt. Not only that, but who knew what damage she might cause to the fossils inside them? And everyone would know about their illicit excursion into a room they weren't even supposed to know about. Matt was getting ready to shout out and stop

her when he noticed something: Jo wasn't on the glass at all. Instead, her weight was resting on the sturdy wooden framework. Relieved, he watched her make it over to the windowsill and reach out for the latch.

The windows were arched and leaded, each piece of the diamond pattern an individual piece of glass. The ancient metal catch didn't budge when she tried to turn it, although the window rattled loosely in its Gothic frame.

'Probably hasn't been opened for years,' she said.

'Or centuries,' put in Matt.

Nevertheless, she tried every one, but with the same result.

'You need something to lever it open.' Matt was already looking round the room. With only moonlight filtering in through the windows, it was impossible to see any small details. 'I'll have a look.'

It needed something really strong to force it open, like a poker, but there was no fireplace. It was hopeless. They were stuck here for the night unless Jo got a phone signal – or, worse – Frank Hellman came back.

Then he saw it. Leaning against the wall in the corner was a long metal hook for opening the small windows high up at the top. In a moment he had grabbed it and handed it up to Jo, who jammed it into the small gap between the window and the frame.

Then Matt carefully clambered up beside her and they both pulled.

When the window swung open, they both almost overbalanced. Suddenly they could feel the cool night air on their faces. Matt and Jo turned and grinned at each other. Then they climbed out.

It wasn't far to the ground, but the gravel they landed on was noisy. Anxious not to immediately attract attention in the morning, Matt pushed the window shut. The catch was now broken and would eventually be noticed, but fortunately the window did not break.

The main thing now was to alert Dad otherwise they would be out here all night.

Jo was fiddling with her phone again. 'I've got signal!' She selected Mr Sharp's mobile number, Matt looking over her shoulder and willing the signal to stay long enough. In their haste to escape from the room, they had hardly thought about how they were going to get back into the castle. It wasn't like Matt not to think of the next move in advance.

Matt heard the phone ring and then his dad's sleepy voice.

'Uncle Alan. We're outside the front door and can't get in. Frank Hellman is here,' Jo explained urgently.

Matt heard the pause as his dad tried to make some sense of this strange message in his half-asleep state.

After a few moments they heard the bolt being drawn on the big front door and then it creaked open, showing Dad's worried face and his tousled hair.

He opened the door wider and Matt and Jo went in. No-one spoke until they were back upstairs in Matt and his dad's room.

'What's this all about?' said Dad as soon as the door was closed. 'You said Hellman was here. Are you sure?'

Matt and Jo both nodded. 'We saw him coming out of the …'

'The dinosaur collection,' finished Jo.

'The what?' Mr Sharp looked bewildered. 'Are you sure?'

Matt knew the first thing they had to do was call the police, but he noticed his dad look at his watch and frown. If they were mistaken, the police would not be happy to have been called at this hour of the night on a wild goose chase.

But it had been Hellman. Matt was sure, and he knew that Jo would back him up.

His dad seemed to make a decision and looked at his phone. He must have had some signal, because he began punching in a number as quickly as he could.

'Inspector Luca Popa,' he said, reading from a piece of paper Matt assumed had been given to him as contact information.

Then he frowned, shook his phone, and clamped it to his ear again. The signal must have returned because someone spoke at the other end. Dad said 'Yes' and ended the call.

'They will be here in ten minutes.'

Matt felt a frisson of excitement at the thought of apprehending Frank Hellman.

This he wouldn't miss for the world.

Wisely, the police did not arrive with sirens and lights blazing, so as not to alert Hellman.

Matt's dad opened the door to greet them. He had insisted that Matt and Jo stay upstairs, much to their disappointment. Despite their efforts to be quiet, somehow the hotel owner had been awoken too. He emerged from behind the stairs, looking perturbed and pushing his arms into a robe.

He spoke sharply to the police as they entered, but it was obvious that he was not going to get the upper hand here. The six police officers spread out and began a search of the castle, ignoring his protestations and asking for keys to be supplied when doors were locked.

Whether or not they had been aware of the dinosaur collection, Matt wasn't sure, but they didn't seem to react.

Before long it was obvious that they had not found Hellman. Their faces showed annoyance and Dad was frowning and looking up to where Matt and Jo were standing on the landing. They retreated into Jo's room.

'He's escaped!' said Jo, rather unnecessarily.

CHAPTER SEVEN

A yellow shaft of moonlight poured in through the window. Jo's room was at the back of the castle, and there were mountains as far as they could see.

They both had the same idea and went to the window. Matt pushed it open and heaved himself onto the windowsill to have a better look. He didn't know what he expected to see apart from forest, and that same churning river, winding away into the distance.

Then he looked down, and the sight almost made him fall back into the room in fear.

On this side, the castle walls were much higher than at the front and backed onto a steep precipice. There was a narrow ledge around the building, but anything falling from that would fall hundreds of feet before reaching the valley below.

'What's the matter?' asked Jo, craning forward for a look.

'Have a look down there.'

She climbed onto the broad sill beside him and they both looked out. The night was cold and the skies clear and scattered with stars.

They were staring down the steep walls of the castle when they spotted a sudden movement. Someone was climbing out of a window directly below. First his bald head emerged and then the rest of his body. He had a heavy backpack on and looked like a grotesque spider as he began to abseil down the castle wall towards the narrow strip of level ground at the edge of the dizzying drop.

They both climbed down from the windowsill and backed away.

Matt could see the whites of Jo's eyes in the moonlight.

'Frank Hellman,' she whispered.

'He's got guts,' Matt said. 'Even the police didn't go round there.'

Just then Matt's dad came in. His face was drawn and dejected and he looked at them both without speaking for a moment or two.

'Have either of you heard the story of the boy who cried "wolf"? And when he was really in danger no-one believed him.'

'Dad, it was him, and we've just seen him abseiling down the castle wall with a heavy pack on his back.' Matt interrupted urgently.

Matt could see that his father didn't believe him. He strolled to the window, already pointing, 'Have you seen out there? It's almost a sheer drop.'

They all looked out but there was no sign of anyone.

'Dad, you have to believe me. It was him, and he's getting away with the eggs! He must be selling them to someone else, and the owner of the hotel must be in on it too.'

'The police are never going to believe us now,

even if I *was* sure. I know you're not lying, but I just doubt what you think you saw.'

'There's only one thing for it then,' said Jo decisively.

They both looked at her.

'We have to go after him ourselves.'

Mr Sharp was shaking his head. 'It's the middle of the night. How can we go after him?'

'Dad, this is *Frank Hellman*, and he's getting away.'

'He must have a vehicle waiting. If you're right, the owner of this place obviously helped him,' Mr Sharp mused.

'And he isn't going to help us find him, Uncle Alan.'

Mr Sharp thought carefully for a moment and then came to a decision. 'In fact, he will do anything to hinder us. He'll have been well paid by Hellman. Put some warm clothes on and let's see what we can find out.'

As Matt thrust his arms into his jacket he wondered just how reckless and futile this idea was. Hellman must have arrived here in a car or van, so where was it now? And they had no car to follow him in.

But once he'd got himself fired up, there was no stopping Dad. Matt saw the gleam in his eyes as they let themselves quietly out of the big front door and crept around the castle to the place where they'd seen Hellman abseil down the wall.

The flat area at the base of the wall was about sixty centimetres wide, then it plunged abruptly down into the valley, far too steep to climb down. So where had Hellman gone?

They walked carefully, hugging the wall. They were fortunate that the moonlight was so bright, although Dad also had a torch – something he always carried on expeditions as part of his kit. The stone wall rose beside them like a cliff and Matt was afraid to look anywhere but straight ahead. This took all his concentration and he planted each foot carefully, thankful that the ground was dry and not slippery.

Dad pointed. 'Here's where he landed.' There were freshly made scuff marks in the earth. 'A brave manoeuvre.'

The slope to their right gradually became less steep until they were able to scramble down to a wooded area. Dad got out his torch and played the beam around the area, walking ahead.

'Here! Look! The grass is trodden down here and some small bushes have been flattened. He

57

is on foot. He's determined. I wouldn't fancy carrying that nest of eggs far though, even in a backpack.'

'What would you do, Dad?'

His dad looked at him. 'Assuming I had done this in the first place, I would probably hide them somewhere and come back when things had quietened down a bit.'

'But what would Frank Hellman do, Uncle Alan?' asked Jo.

'Ah. He would never let them out of his sight.'

They plunged through the forest following Mr Sharp, his torch to the ground. Matt wondered when his dad had found time to become a tracker! He wondered, too, if he knew what to do if they were confronted by a wolf. No-one had mentioned it, but they could still clearly be heard howling at the moon. Matt wondered if Jo had found any advice during her research, but was afraid to even mention the word, as if doing so would conjure up the real thing.

At that moment there was a noise ahead, the sound of someone treading on dry twigs. They all froze, trying to keep their breathing under control. Matt's heart thudded. Was it Hellman? Or was it …?

Then, in a break in the trees, a dark shape

loomed up. A shape larger than a man and certainly larger than a wolf. Matt remembered what other wild animals roamed these forests.

Bears.

CHAPTER EIGHT

Matt felt Jo clasp his arm tightly. He looked towards her but his dad had immediately switched off his torch so that only a little moonlight filtered through from the clearing ahead.

'Don't move!' Jo whispered. 'He might not have seen us.'

Jo had mentioned on another expedition that she knew what to do when confronted by a bear, but at the time Matt had thought she was just showing off. Now he remembered that Jo lived in Canada, where bears were far more of an issue. But did all species of bear behave in the same way? Was the advice the same?

The bear stomped about in the undergrowth and appeared not to have seen them, but it was coming nearer and he had to fight the urge to run. Jo seemed to sense what Matt was thinking and tightened her grip on his arm. He could hear his father trying to control his breathing and wondered whether Jo had him by the arm too.

Once, the bear stopped and stood up straight, looking around.

Had it caught their scent?

After a moment it continued foraging. Apparently they were well enough hidden by the trees.

They stood stock-still for what seemed like hours until at last the bear strolled off. They could hear the sound of its huge paws crashing through the undergrowth long after it had disappeared from sight.

Then Jo released her grip on Matt's arm and they all let out a sigh of relief.

Matt ventured a whisper. 'What do you do if it sees you?'

'You wave your arms slowly above your head and remain calm,' said Jo.

'But whatever you do, you never run or climb a tree. Bears can do those things much better and more quickly than humans.'

Mr Sharp's voice was shaky. 'I forgot about bears,' he said. 'You don't really expect them here in Europe.'

'It was a brown bear,' said Jo, awestruck. 'And a big one.'

They continued on tentatively towards the clearing. The sky was lightening and a few birds were beginning to sing.

Eventually they came to a road and made their way towards a cluster of houses, some of which had lights on as people rose early to begin their day.

Was this where Hellman had come? Matt glanced at his dad's face and saw the look of defeat. He obviously thought they were on a wild goose chase.

They had reached the main street of the village, although no-one seemed to be about yet. A vehicle started up somewhere and became increasingly loud. Instinctively, they retreated around a corner just as a small truck emerged from a side street. It was battered and shabby and the engine sounded rather unhealthy, but it chugged to a standstill outside one of the cottages, facing away from them.

The cottage door opened and a man emerged, carrying a heavy backpack.

Frank Hellman.

Matt heard his dad's sharp intake of breath.

The driver got out and went to the back of the truck where he lowered the tailgate to reveal a large wooden crate with bars on the front. Something was moving about inside but Matt couldn't make out what it was. Hellman and the driver were busy with the crate. Hellman lifted up the backpack and withdrew something from inside, which he placed in the crate.

'It's a dog in there!' said Jo.

'Or a wolf,' Matt heard his dad say. 'He's smuggling them out in a wolf's crate!'

'But where to?' Matt asked.

The two men lifted and fastened the tailgate of the truck and then climbed into the cab.

Without having any clear plan in mind, Matt sprinted up the road and leapt at the back of the truck, grabbing the tailgate. For a moment he felt his feet scraping along the road and thought he was going to be thrown off, but he got a proper grip and hauled himself aboard, hoping that in the dim light of dawn the driver would not see him in the rear-view mirror.

It was a wolf in the crate. Matt could smell it, and the wolf could certainly smell him. It gave a low growl and pawed at the bars. Matt could see that there were two in there, in a crate really only large enough for one. He felt sorry for the animals, but almost smiled when he imagined what Jo's reaction would have been. It was probably better that she wasn't here because she would have jeopardised their position by pounding on the truck roof and demanding the wolves be released. Matt had no plan, though. Why had he gone after Hellman? He had no idea. He wondered where he was going and what Dad and Jo would do now.

He took his phone out of his pocket but there was no signal.

The sun rose and Matt hunkered down beside the crate. The wolves had settled down and he wondered if they had been sedated.

Matt felt drowsy too; he realised that he'd had no sleep at all. He must have drifted off for a while, because suddenly he was woken by a sound that echoed through the countryside.

A police siren. He looked up and saw flashing lights approaching from behind them and gaining rapidly.

The driver had become aware of them too, and the truck lurched forward in a burst of speed, wavering across the road a little. Matt clung on, just as he had in the cart that had given them a lift to the hotel.

But the modern police car was gaining on the old truck fast and Matt sat up and waved frantically. The truck lurched again and he grabbed at the side. The wolves had awoken too, and he saw the look of fear in their eyes.

Matt looked ahead and saw that they were approaching a tight bend in the road. A bend that they couldn't possibly manage at this speed.

With a squeal of brakes, the truck tipped onto two wheels, teetered there for a moment, and then keeled right over onto its side. Matt leapt out of the back and landed on a grassy slope, then continued to roll until a tree stopped him with a jolt. He lay there for a moment, gasping for breath and wondering if he was hurt. After a quick assessment of the situation, he decided that he would just have a big bruise on his side where he had hit the tree.

He was just about to get up when he heard a sound from near his left ear.

A growl.

He looked round. The two wolves had escaped from their broken crate and were standing over him, teeth bared and lips curled.

CHAPTER NINE

Matt didn't know what to do. Should he play dead? Should he make a lot of noise? Maybe he should stand up and show how big he was, like you were supposed to with bears. Or should he just keep still?

He had no idea.

The two wolves continued to watch him, their heads thrust forward, growling softly. Beautiful creatures. Even in his fear, he was struck by their magnificent coats.

It seemed that their attention had begun to wander. Now and again one would look up and sniff the air. They were certainly preoccupied with something.

Matt took a chance and began slowly to get to his feet. One of them took a step back.

He began to talk to them softly, and wondered whether they remembered him from the truck and associated him with their imprisonment.

Then there was a movement behind them; up the hill towards the road he could see Dad and Jo accompanied by two policemen.

One of the policemen said something and indicated that Matt should slowly walk towards them. Keeping an eye on the wolves, he clambered carefully up the hill. The wolves followed at the same pace, but stopped short of the humans. Matt ran into his dad's arms.

'You're safe, Matt,' Dad whispered.

'Wolves rarely attack humans,' said Jo soberly.

'That's not very reassuring when you have two of them leaning over you baring their teeth,' Matt retorted irritably.

'It must have been scary,' Jo added, looking suitably contrite.

'Have they got Hellman?' asked Matt.

Dad shook his head. 'He escaped into the forest, but we have recovered the eggs. They were hidden in the false bottom of the wolf crate. Who would look in there?'

They walked back up to the road.

'Are you all right, Matt?' said his dad. 'You just flew off that truck!'

Matt nodded. 'Just bruised. Where was Hellman going with the wolves?'

'We don't know yet,' said his dad. 'No-one is talking at the moment, but the truck driver has been arrested as an accomplice. We flagged down a patrol car but it took us a while to convince the police that we really had seen Hellman after last night's perceived false alarm. It was only when I insisted on speaking on their radio to a senior officer who spoke English that things happened quickly.'

While the search went on for Hellman, the police drove them back to the hotel and arranged for someone from a garage to pick up their car and fix the tyre.

The hotel owner opened the door to them resignedly. Matt supposed it couldn't be proved that he had been Hellman's accomplice, but surely he would be questioned as to where he had obtained his fossils. Was it illegal to have a private collection?

The door to the exhibit room was open and the three of them walked in. It was much more impressive in daylight.

Mr Sharp stood at the door, speechless. It was one thing to see these fossils in a museum but quite another to see them in a private home. Then he strode forward, past the large skeleton in the centre of the room, to a smaller one about the size of a horse.

'Balaur,' he said. 'Known as the stocky dragon.'

'And here's a Hatzegopteryx, Dad.' Matt had hardly recognised the great flying reptile without its flesh. He remembered what it had looked like in his vision. And what it had felt like.

'I can touch things in my visions now, Jo,' he said, and she turned and grinned at him, sharing his excitement.

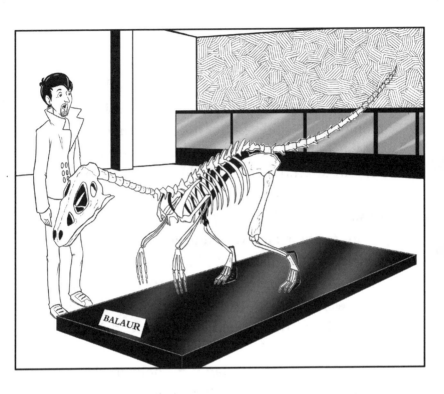

'The last vision I had was of one of these and I reached out and touched its tough scaly skin. Isn't that awesome?' It felt good to confide in her now. Matt knew that she shared his enthusiasm.

'You touched it?' said a voice behind them. It was the hotel owner, who had followed them in.

'In a dream,' said Matt, quickly. 'I'm always dreaming of dinosaurs.' He wasn't ready to share his visions with the world yet, especially not with this man, although he knew they wouldn't be able to keep it a secret for much longer.

'Frank left a message for you,' he said, a smug smile on his face. He pretended to think for a moment. 'He said: "Better luck next time".'

Matt felt his father tense, but he said nothing. The fossil room had suddenly lost its appeal and they brushed past the hotel owner and went upstairs to get their things.

Before their car was returned, the policeman who spoke English came back to tell them that although they had failed to apprehend Hellman, they were grateful to have recovered the eggs. When they questioned the truck driver, he admitted that Hellman had a contract with a landowner in Scotland to deliver the two wolves as he was planning to reintroduce them into the country. This transaction, as far as the Romanians were concerned, was above board and legal, but Frank had cleverly had crates made with false bottoms to smuggle out the eggs. They were bound for a private collector in the north of England.

Mr Sharp sighed and shook his head. 'I'm sorry we didn't get him, but at least we could help keep the eggs in the country.' He looked at Matt and Jo. 'And I have a lot of thinking to do before I allow you on another expedition. I hadn't expected that it would put our lives in danger.'

Matt felt disappointed, but the feeling soon went. He was sure he'd be able to persuade his dad when another expedition was planned.

It seemed that Hellman had not wanted to draw attention to himself by hiring a car. He had planned the whole operation and paid drivers along the way, including the man who had made the specially adapted crate.

Eventually Mr Sharp, Matt and Jo made it back to Bucharest, where they revisited the Grigore Antipa Museum and Matt's dad was able to spend as much time as he wanted admiring the Deinotherium giganteum. As they were leaving, the curator came to thank them. He had a present for Mr Sharp to donate to a museum in the UK. It was one of the fossils from the castle.

They all tried to guess what it was, though they didn't risk opening it until they reached Matt's house.

Back in the living room at home, Matt and Jo watched eagerly as Mr Sharp opened the wrapping and carefully peeled back the bubble wrap. A small fossilised egg lay in his hand. Matt's dad gave a knowing smile as he handed it to him, and then he and Jo watched intently as Matt enclosed the egg with both hands and closed his eyes.

The vision came on quickly this time, taking him by surprise. Before he knew it he was there, in the marshy landscape, and in front of him stood the strangest creature he had ever seen. It looked like something someone had put together using odd parts from several other creatures.

As he stared at it, it suddenly kicked out at him with one powerful back leg, which made Matt leap backwards. Wow! A kick-boxer. Was that how it attacked its prey? Did that mean it was a carnivore? Was this a Balaur?

It had a medium-sized head with a heavy jaw containing lots of teeth, but in other ways it looked like a weird bird. A giant, thickset and chunky bird about two metres long.

Although it had appeared to kick at him, he knew that it couldn't see him. There must be something standing right where he was.

Matt backed away a little and there it was, pinned under that horrendous claw. A small, lizard-like reptile that had no chance against this heavyweight. The hind claw had two sickle-shaped claws as part of its armoury. Lethal weapons.

Tentatively, Matt reached out to touch the claw, running his finger carefully along its sharp edge.

The front limbs were smaller and had what looked like primitive wings. The tail fanned out towards the distal end.

Matt looked around. So this was Hateg Island; in seventy million years this would be Romania. Sea levels had been much higher during the time he could see in this vision, and much of Europe was covered in water.

As the scene faded and Matt came back to the present, his dad said, 'Was I right?'

'I think it was Balaur bondoc,' said Matt. 'Is that what you guessed, Dad?'

His dad nodded. 'It's never been found anywhere else, and they have never found a skull so they don't know whether it was a carnivore or herbivore.'

'Well, it certainly had a powerful kick and lethal claws on its back legs.'

'Like a cassowary,' said Jo. 'They strike with a claw on their feet.'

'Yes, but cassowaries are herbivores. They defend their young with that claw but they don't eat the victim,' Mr Sharp said.

'I can't be sure with the Balaur, but it had lots of teeth and looked as though it was about to eat its prey.' Matt reached for a piece of paper and a pencil. 'Let me draw it while it's still in my mind. You've never seen such a strange creature!'

The door opened and Matt's mum and sister, Beth, came in.

'Did you really see a wolf?' asked Beth, wide-eyed.

'Yes, and we also saw a bear,' said Matt. He did his best bear impersonation. 'Grrrr!'

Everyone laughed, but Matt's encounters

with the wildlife of Romania were not things he wanted to think about too much. The memories were too fresh in his mind and it would be a while before he forgot those snarling faces so close to his.

But it hadn't put him off. Nothing could stop him from going on these expeditions, and he wondered where the next one would take them.